To Siân, my baby sister S.L-J.

For my mum and her baby brother (Uncle George) D.R.

First published 2017 by Walker Books Ltd
87 Vauxhall Walk, London SE11 5HJ

10 9 8 7 6 5 4 3 2 1

Text © 2017 Sally Lloyd-Jones
Illustrations © 2017 David Roberts

The right of Sally Lloyd-Jones and David Roberts to be identified as author
and illustrator respectively of this work has been asserted by them in
accordance with the Copyright, Designs and Patents Act 1988

This book has been set in Avenir

Printed in China

British Library Cataloguing in Publication Data: a catalogue for this book is
available from the British Library

ISBN 978-1-4063-2466-2

www.walker.co.uk

WALKER BOOKS
AND SUBSIDIARIES
LONDON • BOSTON • SYDNEY • AUCKLAND

HIS ROYAL TINYNESS

A Terrible True Story

Sally Lloyd-Jones

Pictures by
David Roberts

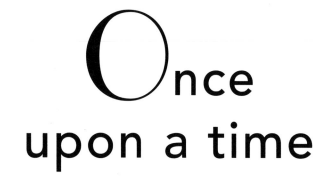

Once
upon a time

there was a Happy Family…

A mum

A dad

A gerbil

And the most beautifulest, cleverest, ever-so-kindest
Princess with long flowing wondrous hair.
(In fact, actually, she is
ME!)

They all lived happily together in The Land where there was always time for stories, plenty of room on your mum's lap and absolutely NEVER any screaming.

Until one horrible, NO GOOD day, when a new ruler was born...

Behold ~
His Royal Highness, King Baby!

No sooner had the baby arrived than suddenly
there was no talk in all The Land except:

"Such a nice big BURP!" and, "Oh what a lovely POO-POO!"

completely NON-STOP ALL THE TIME!

It came to pass that the baby, instead of going away,
only grew fatter.

And even fatter still… He got a tooth… And a bit of hair…

Behold
The Royal
Tooth

And after A WHOLE ENTIRE YEAR of his Wicked Rule,
the Tragical Day arrived…

The King's First Birthday!

At the very stroke of 6.15 o'clock,
the darling Princess was woken by the rude
and very awful shouty-shrieking of...

The Darling Birthday Boy!
Ruler of the Land!
His Royal Tinyness, King Baby!

The gentle girl (lovely in all her ways) had to
cook her own breakfast – ALONE BY HERSELF –
like a poor orphan child. But meanwhile...

BEHOLD His Royal Hungriness,
His Really-Rather-Greediness!
His Royal Roundness, King Baby!

After breakfast,
the cruelly-mistreated
Princess hardly
even got a turn
in the bathroom.
But meanwhile…

BEHOLD *His Royal*
Clean-and-Sparklyness!
(What a Smelly!)
King Baby.

Then the kind-hearted girl (as beautiful as a spring flower), clothed only in a raggedy old dress (that she had grown out of ages ago), was turned by her cruel-almost-stepmother into a servant and had to tidy up her WHOLE ENTIRE bedroom with completely no help from anybody.

But meanwhile...

BEHOLD *Majesty Boy!*
(Such a sight to see!)
His Almost Perfectness, King Baby.

Next, the tender girl (of such delicate, dainty feet) was
made to march o'er all the shops, carrying enormous bags
so her arms almost fell off. And then she was forced to run BEHIND
the Splendid Carriage – wherein rested The Royal Bottom…

BEHOLD! *His One-and-Only Spoiltness, King Baby!*

From Far and Wide, at last, the Royal Guests arrived.
His Lordships, Her Ladyships, Their Grandpa-and-Grandma-ships,
His Uncle-ships, Her Aunty-ships, and even Their Furry Pet-ships.

They came, bearing gifts! Kneeling before him! Kissing his toes!
Speaking only in Nonsense! *"Bubba-Dubba-Wub!"* *"Ickle-Tickle-
Pickle-Poo!"* *"Wispsy-Wopsy-Woo!"*

The Whole Land was under an Enchantment!
She had become an invisible girl in her own home.
What could the poor innocent Princess do?

The Princess knew EXACTLY!

She would come to the party disguised as …
a Mysterious Fairy,
with a magic wand,
a big very magical nose,
and a cunning plan…

It was time to break the spell!
She would tell all The Land
the terrible TRUE story!

The Mysterious Fairy took a deep breath…

"Once Upon A Time..."

But before she could even begin
there appeared a Giant Cake
of Chocolate with candles on top!
Everyone was singing!
The King was crowned:

Happy Birthday to HIM!
Happy Birthday to HIM!
Happy Birthday Dear ...

(His-Really-Annoying-Boringness) ...
Happy Birthday to HIM!

Scarcely had these words been sung, when ...

HARK!

A Royal Scream echoed around The Palace.

BEHOLD

His Royal Unhappiness!
With Royal Drool all dribbling down!

WAAAAAAA-O-E-E-AAARGH!

His Lordships,
Her Ladyships,
Their Grandpa-and-Grandma-ships,
His Uncle-ships,
Her Aunty-ships,
and even Their Furry Pet-ships swooped,
and dabbed, and wiped, and mopped.

"Oh dear!" they cried.
"Who didn't have their nap?"
"Off to Bed!"
"Say Night-Night!"
"Wave Bye-Bye!"

His poor Birthday Highness only screamed louder.
And even LOUDER still…

He kicked his legs!

He thumped his fists!

He shook his head!

He threw down ...

His Orb! His Sceptre! His Royal Crown!

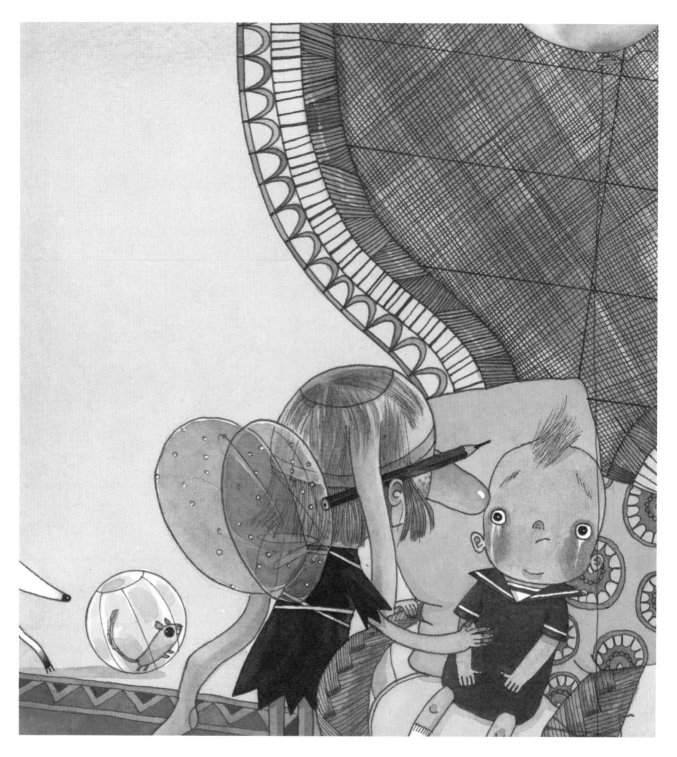

Despite all that had Befallen her, the Kind Fairy's loveliness had grown ever stronger (like a sparkling mountain stream). She would rescue him! "Don't cry, Mr Baby," she whispered in his ear.

And she kissed his cheek.

IN AN INSTANT his screaming was cured!

He smiled, and giggled, and pointed at her ugly nose.

"My Brother and Me must do our Colouring NOW!" the Fairy
declared to All The Land. "We are leaving WITHOUT DELAY!"

And so they did. Together. Holding hands.

But not before the little King issued a Royal Decree:

"Blupp dob Bip? Op nopp!!"

(Which is Baby for, "BEHOLD!
My Favourite and My Best Princess Big Sister
EVER in the whole WORLD!" Basically.)

And the end of the story is:

They Lived Happily Ever After

THE END.

A mum

A dad

A gerbil

A brother

And the most beautifulest, cleverest, ever-so-kindest,
Princess Big Sister, with long flowing wondrous hair.

(PS: The King was too little to eat his birthday cake so, out of the goodness of her heart, the Princess ate his piece for him.)